USBORNE HOTSHOTS
TRAVEL GAMES

USBORNE HOTSHOTS
TRAVEL GAMES

Tony Potter and Moira Butterfield

Edited by Alastair Smith
Designed by Fiona Johnson

Illustrated by Iain Ashman,
Kim Blundell, Chris Lyon
and Guy Smith

Series editor: Judy Tatchell
Series designer: Ruth Russell

CONTENTS

- 4 Games for any journey
- 21 The great air quiz
- 22 Special games for car journeys
- 29 The big car quiz
- 30 Puzzle answers
- 32 How to make a scorer

You can play most of the games in this book on any journey, whether in a car, train, plane or boat. Some of the games, though, are specially designed for playing on a car journey.

You need to take the things below to be able to play some of the games. It is a good idea to pack them in one small bag.

Tear-off notepad for scoring
Pencils
Drawing pad
Reusable adhesive, such as BLU-TACK™.
Dice or scorer

Many of the games in this book require you to use a dice. If you don't have a dice you can make a scorer. You can find out how to make one on page 32.

Games for any journey

Treasure hunt

A competition has been organized by the *Daily Blab* newspaper. The two finalists (one in a red car, one in a yellow car) have to follow some clues to find some treasure. They must always drive at 30kmph (20mph).

By following the clues and reading the map, can you say where the treasure is and guess who gets there first? When you get home you could measure their journeys from the map, to check the distances. You can find out how to measure the map at the top of the next page.

Map key:
- City
- Village
- Road
- Railway
- River
- Beach
- Nature park
- Airport
- Mansion

Red car starts here

Locations on map: Rougeville, Bigsville, Forest Green, Smugglers Cove, Sandybay Village, Trainsend, Rich Mansion

Compass: North, East, South, West

Clues

1. Drive to the nearest city, Bigsville.

2. Take the road south, then turn left at the junction.

3. Fork right at the first sign of nature.

4. Cross a river, then enter a village.

5. Go south, crossing the river again.

6. Pass some planes and then head west.

7. Cross a railway line.

8. Take the fork toward the water.

9. Go to the village close to a beach.

10. Drive to the nearest mansion.

Measuring a map

Try to measure as accurately as you can.

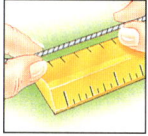

Your measurement will depend on the scale of the map.

1. Hold some thread along the line of the road between two points on the route.

2. Hold the thread tight against the scale of the map and read off the distance.

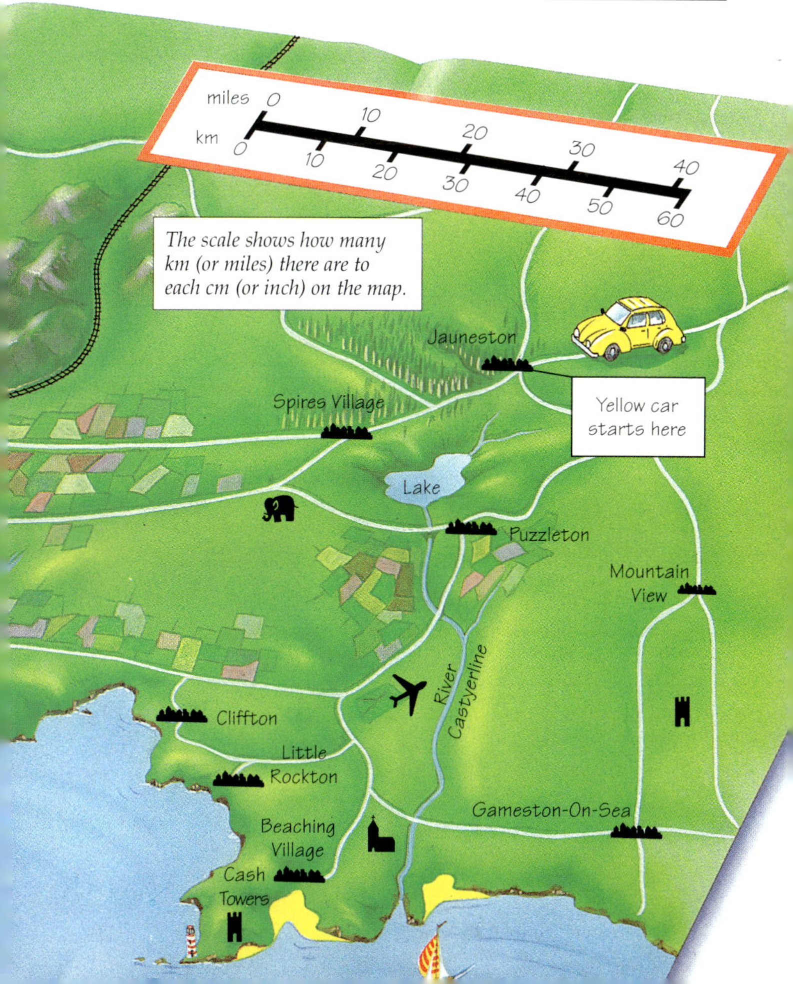

miles 0 — 10 — 20 — 30 — 40
km 0 — 10 — 20 — 30 — 40 — 50 — 60

The scale shows how many km (or miles) there are to each cm (or inch) on the map.

Jauneston

Yellow car starts here

Spires Village

Lake

Puzzleton

Mountain View

River Castyerline

Cliffton

Little Rockton

Gameston-On-Sea

Beaching Village

Cash Towers

Buy a car for Sam Snoop

Secret agent Sam Snoop is being pursued by enemy agents. His ESD (Enemy Spy Detector) tells him that his rivals are exactly 50km (30 miles) behind, driving at 150kmph (90mph).

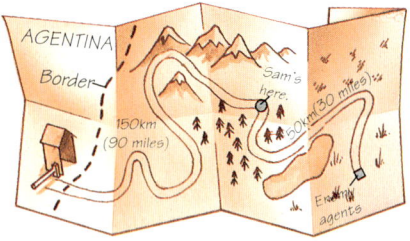

Unfortunately, Sam's car has broken down 150km (90 miles) from the border of Agentina, the nearest safe country for him. However, he is near "Slippery Stan's Auto Heaven", a second-hand car dealer's. Of the five cars on offer, which one should Sam choose?

Blue Bird. Goes at 50kmph (30mph). Engine stops after 30 minutes.

Old Faithful. All wheels drop off if driven over 150kmph (90mph).

Green Grumbler. Only has reverse gear. Reverses at 100kmph (60mph).

Tangerine Dream. Top speed 150kmph (90mph). Needs new spark plugs every 15 minutes. These take 15 minutes to fit.

Fireball. Does 300kmph (180mph). Only works for 20 minutes.

Hint
Calculate how long the enemy spies take to reach the border, then determine how long each of Slippery Stan's cars would take.

Decide the distance

This blue car takes three minutes at 30kmph (20mph) to reach the top of the hill and three minutes at twice the speed to reach the bottom. How far has it gone by the time it reaches the bottom of the hill?

Choose the route

Parcel Pete has to deliver packages to each of the ten houses shown in this picture. To ensure a fast service, can you see where he should start and the route he should take to avoid driving down any street more than once?

Fast Freddie's car

Fast Freddie has an old car which is always needing new parts. These cost Freddie a fortune. In his country the currency is splots. Can you calculate how much Freddie spends on spare parts for every 10,000km (6,000 miles) he drives?

Two fan belts every 2,000km (1,200 miles). Two splots each.

One air filter every 100km (60 miles). One splot each.

One can of oil every 500km (300 miles). Ten splots each.

Three wheels every 1000km (600 miles). Twenty splots each.

Six spark plugs every 500km (300 miles). Five splots each.

Micky's rebuild

Mechanical Micky rebuilt his old car. However, when he did the job, he changed some of the details. Comparing the two pictures, can you spot 16 things that Micky left off when he rebuilt the car?

Before the rebuild

After the rebuild

Customs officer game

People arriving from other countries have to a pay tax (called "duty") if they bring certain goods into the country. A customs officer's job is to catch any people who try to avoid paying tax. In this game for three or more people, each player takes a turn as a customs officer. Use an imaginary currency (we've used splots) for the value of the goods. Before you start, copy the tickets shown at the top of the next page and put them in a bag.

How to play

His duty adds up to 30 splots really.

1. One player is the customs officer, the others are the passengers. One passenger closes his eyes and takes three goods tickets from the bag.

2. The passenger adds up the duty and tells the officer how much is owed. If more than 25 splots is owed, he should pretend that he has less.

3. The officer demands to see the tickets if he thinks a lie has been told. If he is right, the officer scores ten points.

4. He loses five points if his challenge is wrong. After each turn the tickets are put back in the bag and the officer notes his score.

5. Each passenger has two turns at picking tickets. Then they choose a new customs officer until everyone has taken a turn.

6. Whoever scores the most points as customs officer is the winner. Be careful, you could score less than zero!

Making your goods tickets

Make your goods tickets by copying these little pictures onto pieces of paper. Put all the finished tickets in a bag.

Smuggler search

Notorious Norbert is wanted for smuggling goods through ports and airports around the world. His picture is shown here on a "Wanted" poster.

Max Penalty, an eagle-eyed customs officer, has stopped four passengers. Their passport photos are shown on the right. Max suspects that one of them is Norbert wearing a cunning disguise. Which person should he arrest on suspicion of being the sneaky smuggler?

Air race game

This race is for two players. The winner is the first to get their plane from Fogsville to Cloudsville. You need dice or a scorer (see page 32), and two counters to use as planes. Make one each by writing your name on a slip of paper. You might need to play this game on a table, so it's best for a train or plane journey. You could hold your counters in place using reusable adhesive*.

How to play

1. Put your counter on a start square. Take turns throwing the dice or spinning the scorer. Move your plane the number of squares thrown.

2. Start by flying along the route that leads from your start square. Then follow the instructions printed on the squares that you land on.

3. If you are both on the same route and you throw a number which would land you on the same square as another plane, you cannot move.

4. You must land on the same route that you started on. In order to land, you must throw the exact number that you require.

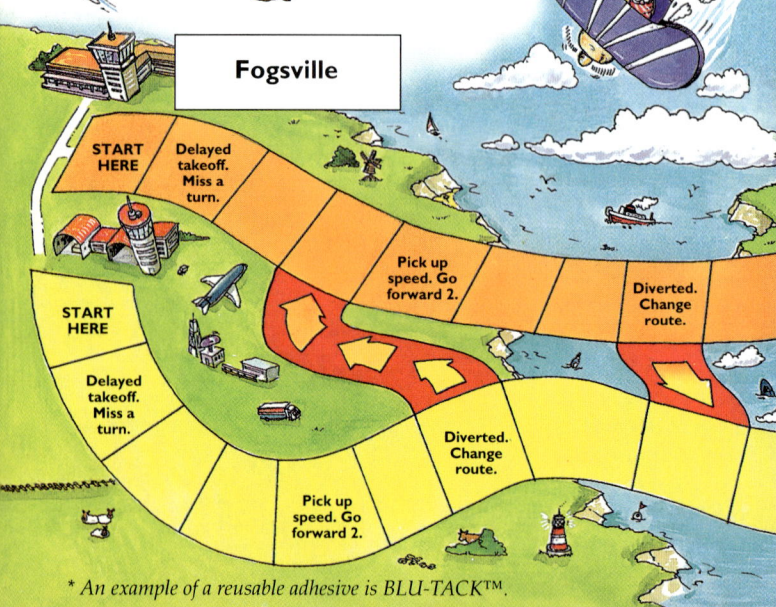

An example of a reusable adhesive is BLU-TACK™.

Pyramid puzzle

How did this display team make the second pyramid from the first by moving only three acrobats?

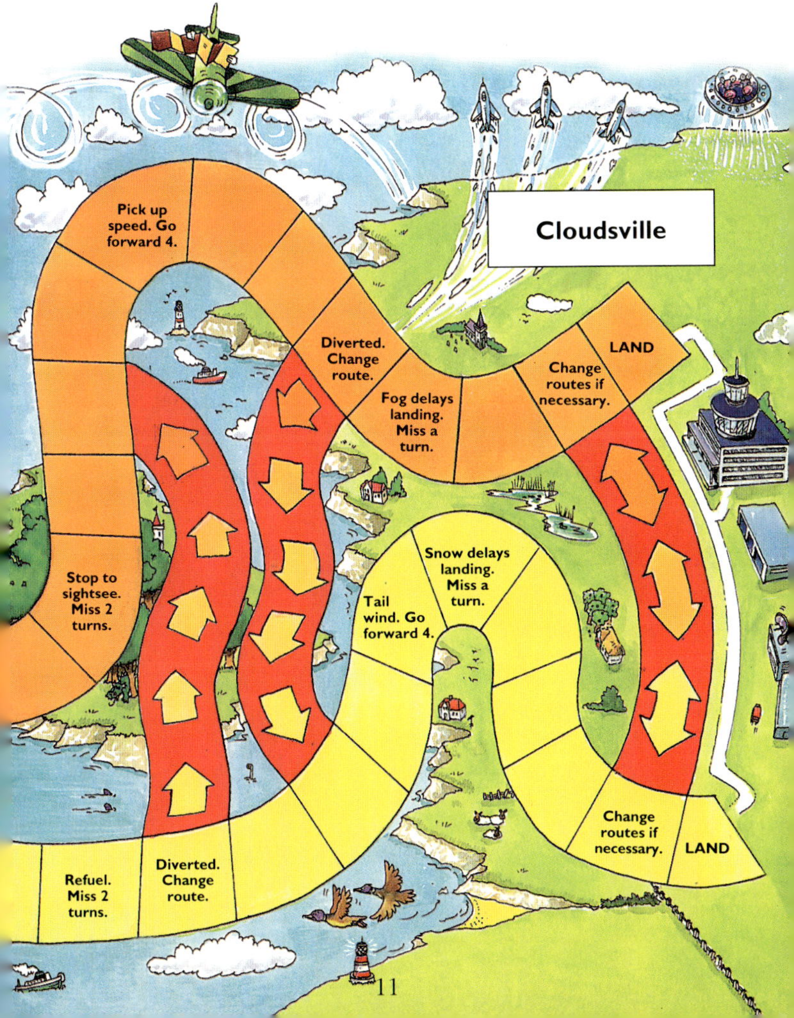

Cloudsville

- Pick up speed. Go forward 4.
- Diverted. Change route.
- Fog delays landing. Miss a turn.
- LAND
- Change routes if necessary.
- Stop to sightsee. Miss 2 turns.
- Snow delays landing. Miss a turn.
- Tail wind. Go forward 4.
- Change routes if necessary.
- LAND
- Refuel. Miss 2 turns.
- Diverted. Change route.

Sneaky spies

This picture shows a sticky moment in the life of top secret agent Sam Snoop. He wants to catch a plane home, but several enemy spies are out to get him before he can board his plane. Which way should Sam go through the airport so that he avoids the spies and catches his plane?

Sam Snoop

Spot the spies

See if you can spot how many spies are lurking at the airport, trying to catch Sam Snoop.

All the spies are dressed the same. This is what they look like.

Passport pieces

Here is Madame LeRich's passport picture. To the right of it are some cut up pieces of pictures. Can you work out which of the cut up pieces on the right belong to the passport picture on the left?

Picture

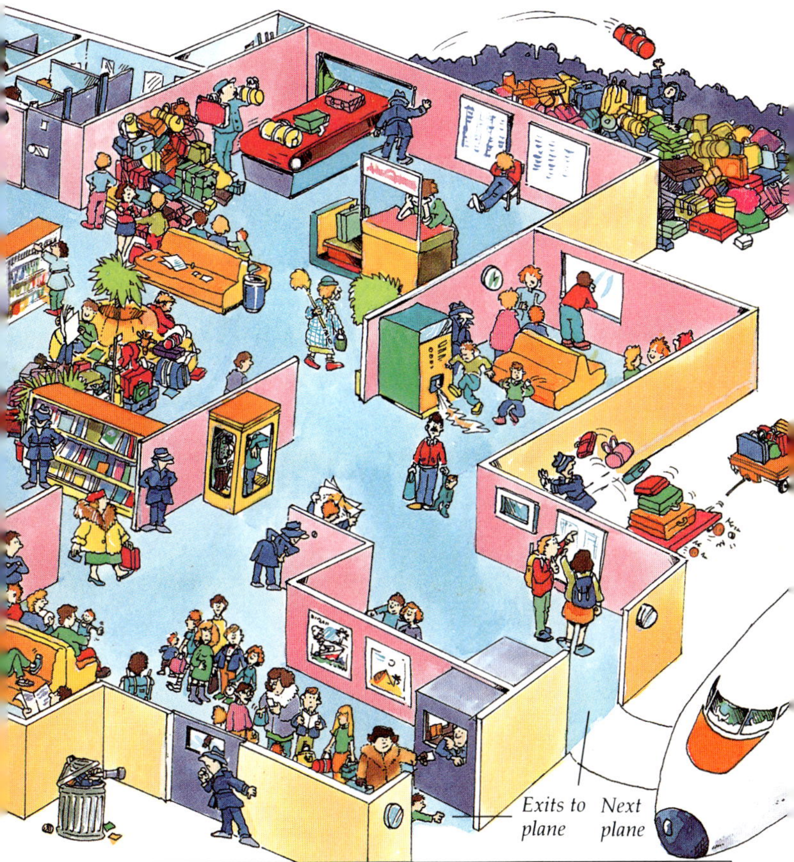
Exits to plane
Next plane

The professor's prototypes

Here are five useless designs by Professor Headwind, the chief designer at Mugsair, a small aircraft company. Which one will have the most trouble landing?

1
2
3
4
5

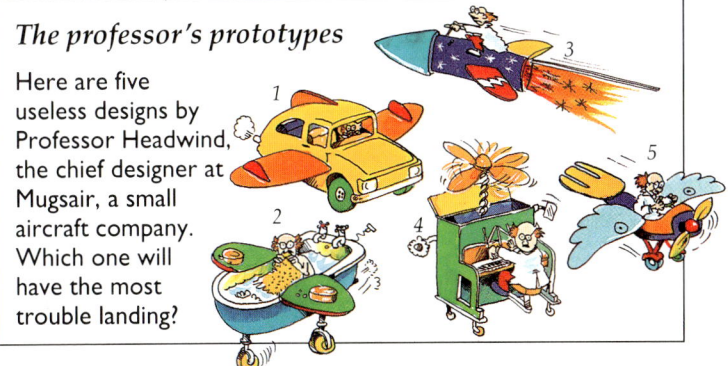

Takeoff race

This is a game of luck for two players or more. The idea of the game is to imagine that you have a plane each. See which of you can load all the cargo onto your plane first and then take off.

How to play

1. Take turns throwing a dice or spinning a scorer. Look at the pictures on the right to see what cargo you can load for each number you throw.

2. Notice that you have to collect more than one of some of the items in order to fill your plane. For example, you need to collect two luggage containers, so you will need to throw two twos.

3. When you have loaded all the items you must throw a six to take off.

4. The player who takes off first wins the game. It is a good idea to keep a list of items as you load them, as shown below.

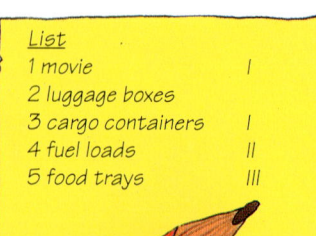

In-flight movie.
Load one.

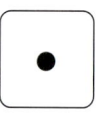 

Luggage container.
Load two.

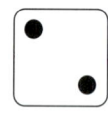 

Cargo container.
Load three.

 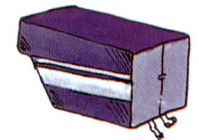

Fuel load.
Load four.

Food tray.
Load five.

Throw a six to take off.

Clear to land

Planes must wait for permission to land at busy airports by flying in circles at different levels. This is called "stacking". As soon as the plane at the lowest level lands, those above it can drop to the next level in the stack. This game is a race to land for two players.

How to play

1. Choose a stack each. Take turns to throw a dice or spin a scorer. Start with your finger on the top level of your stack.

2. Move down to the next level only when you have thrown the number of the level that you are on.

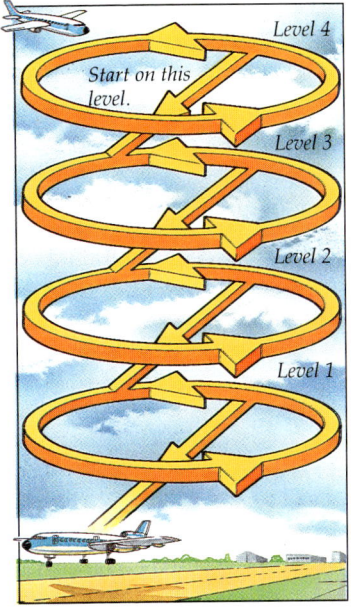
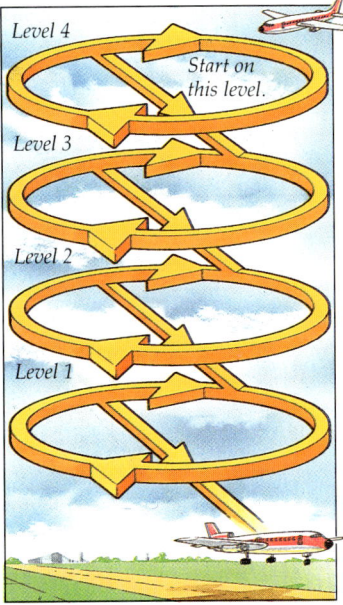

Level 4
Score a four to move down a level.

Level 3
Score a three to move down a level.

Level 2
Score a two to move down a level.

Level 1
Score a one in order to land.

Memory car

Look at this picture of car parts for 30 seconds and then close the book. In two minutes write down as many things as you can remember. Score 1 point for each correct item, but lose 2 points for anything you remember wrongly.

Consequences

To play this game you need a piece of paper and a pen or pencil for each player. You need at least two people.

How to play

1. Everyone writes a name at the top of their paper. Then fold the paper over, to conceal the name. Pass your paper to the person next to you.

2. Continue by writing things which fit the phrases shown below, folding the papers and passing them on each time.

3. Finally, unfold the papers and read them out, using the phrases on the left to make sentences for each section.

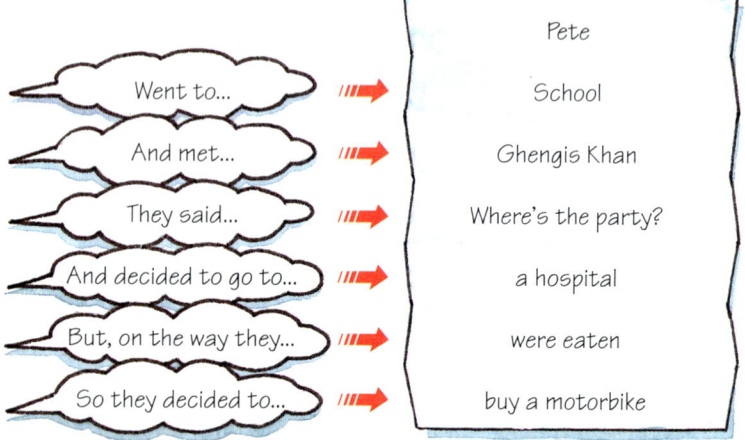

Banana drama

This game is great to play on any journey.

How to play

1. One person (who is known as the guesser) covers her ears and closes her eyes. Then everyone else picks a verb between them. (Verbs are "doing" words, such as run, jump, sleep, sit, sneeze and so on.)

2. Get the guesser to uncover her ears and open her eyes when the verb has been agreed. Then she has to find out the chosen word by asking questions, changing the verb in the question to "banana". For example, she could ask, "Do you banana in a car?" or "Am I bananaring right now?"

3. The guesser scores 1 point for every question she asked before guessing the word. When all players have had a turn at being the guesser, compare your scores. The lowest scorer wins.

Who lives there?

With this game you can really let your imagination run riot. Take turns describing the owners of unusual houses seen on a journey. Imagine what they look like, what food they like, the pets they keep and so on.

Alphabet memory game

Take turns saying what you want to eat. The first person chooses something beginning with "A". The next person says what the first person said and adds something beginning with "B", and so on until you get to "Z". If you make a mistake you are out. The person who recites the longest list wins.

I'm so hungry I could eat an apple.

I'm so hungry I could eat an apple and a bus.

I'm so hungry I could eat an apple, a bus and a chilli.

Collect the cases

This is a race for two players, to see who can collect their baggage first from one of these airport conveyor belts.

How to play

1. Each player needs a small counter to play. You could make them if you like (see page 26 for instructions).*

2. Choose a conveyor belt each. The player on the left collects all the numbered yellow cases. The player on the right collects all the numbered red cases.

3. Take turns throwing a dice or spinning a scorer. Move your counter the number of squares you have thrown. When you land on a bag, note its number.

4. The winner is the first person to collect all the numbered baggage from his conveyor belt.

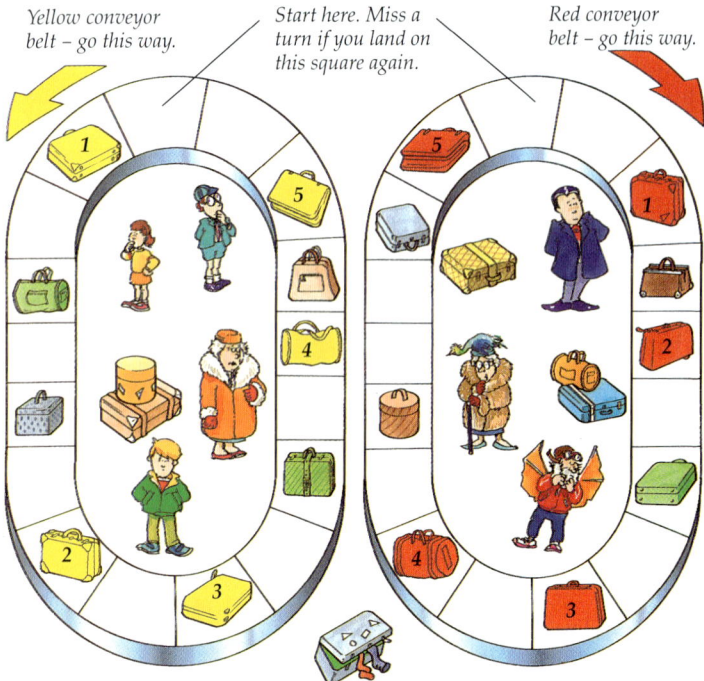

Yellow conveyor belt – go this way.

Start here. Miss a turn if you land on this square again.

Red conveyor belt – go this way.

* *You can stick counters to playing boards with reusable adhesive, such as BLU-TACK*™.

Fill the food tray

The idea of this game is for you to be a super-efficient flight attendant and collect as many things as you can to fill an airline food tray.

How to play

1. Use small counters to play.

2. Take turns throwing a dice or spinning a scorer. Move your counter along the row the number of spaces thrown. When you get to the end of a row follow the arrow to move down to the next one.

3. Collect the objects by landing on them. Make a note of the things that you collect.

4. If you land on a space which says you can go up or down, you can move to a different row and try to collect items that you have not yet collected.

5. When you land on the "finish" square you cannot move any more. You must throw the exact number you need to land on the "finish" square. When you have both finished the one with the fullest tray wins.

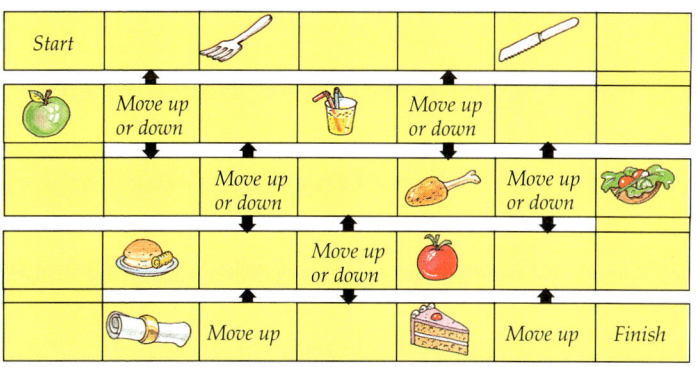

Plane maze

These people are guiding planes to parking bays, using batons to make signals for pilots to follow.

MOVE AHEAD   TURN RIGHT   TURN LEFT   STOP!

Look at the signals shown below. Can you see which bay the plane is being directed to in the picture beneath the signals?

Parking problem

Three planes have been allocated runways at Fogsville airport. The runways should match the planes. Can you figure out how to move them along the connecting paths (called taxiways) to their runways, without them meeting or parking on the same runway?

The great air quiz

There are three suggested answers to each of these questions. Write down the question number, then the letter of the answer you think is correct. You could try doing this quiz with other people. The person with the highest score wins.

1. Who was Orville Wright?

a. *The tallest ever pilot.*
b. *The pilot of the first plane.*
c. *World baggage handling champion, 1963.*

2. Who was Louis Blériot?

a. *The first flight attendant.*
b. *A famous airline chef.*
c. *The first person to fly the English Channel.*

3. What is a Zeppelin?

a. *An airship.*
b. *A German sausage sandwich invented by Louis Blériot.*
c. *The round part of a jet engine.*

4. What is an altimeter?

a. *A type of air sickness pill.*
b. *An automatic pilot device.*
c. *A device for measuring how high a plane is flying.*

5. What is an airbridge?

a. *A game of cards.*
b. *A tightrope between two planes.*
c. *A passage that links a plane to an airport terminal.*

6. What is a biplane?

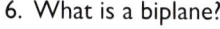

a. *A striped plane.*
b. *A plane with double wings.*
c. *A computerized plane.*

7. Where is Orly airport?

a. *Orlando, USA.*
b. *The Bahamas.*
c. *Paris, France.*

8. What is Chicago O'Hare airport famous for?

a. *It sells the biggest hamburgers in the world.*
b. *It is the busiest airport in the world.*
c. *It was built in 1744.*

9. What do aircraft designers use a wind tunnel for?

a. *To help them figure out a plane's shape.*
b. *Cleaning a plane.*
c. *Drying their hair.*

10. When was the first ever plane flight?

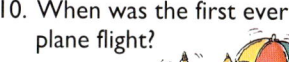

a. *1903.*
b. *1744.*
c. *1960.*

Special games for car journeys

Suitcase

The idea of this game is to spot certain things out of the window while you're on a car journey.

How to play

1. Each player chooses ten things from the picture shown below and makes a list of their choices. It doesn't matter if some choices are the same as those of other players. Next, draw a picture beside each item, to make a list like the one on the right.

2. Spot things beginning with the same letter (or letters if the item's name contains two words, such as a teddy bear). If you wanted to cross the teddy bear off your list you would then have to spot, for example, a truck badge or a tall building.

3. Appoint one passenger to be the judge. The judge's job is to check the names of the things that you spot and to tell you whether or not they are allowed.

4. Call "Suitcase!" when you spot something and tell everyone what it is. If the judge says that you have spotted something correctly then you can tick the item on your list.

5. The winner is the first person to tick everything on their list. For longer journeys you could make longer lists.

Verrroom!

For this game you need a copy of the speedometer below for each player. You then shade it in, 5 or 10 kmph (or mph) at a time, by being the first to say "VERRROOM!" when you spot something from the charts underneath. The first to reach 100 is the winner.

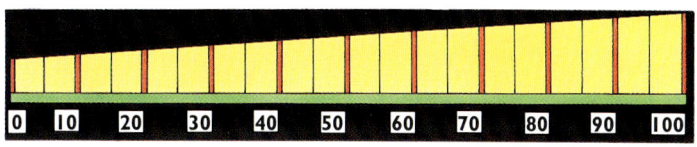

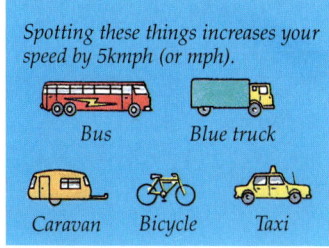

Spotting these things increases your speed by 5kmph (or mph).

Bus Blue truck
Caravan Bicycle Taxi

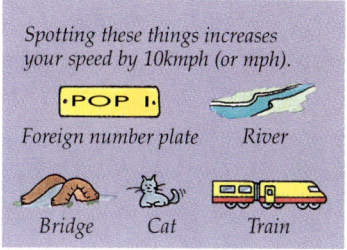

Spotting these things increases your speed by 10kmph (or mph).

Foreign number plate River
Bridge Cat Train

Wildlife collection

The idea of this game is to be the first to collect a herd of imaginary wild animals.

How to play

1. First draw ten wild animals. Then decide what objects you need to spot in order to collect your animals. The notebook on the right gives some ideas. For example, a park bench could count as an elephant, a policeman as a tiger and so on.

2. You collect an animal by being the first to spot its object and call out the animal's name. It escapes if you call it by the wrong name, but can be captured by someone else. The first person to collect all the animals wins the game.

Exhausts and antennas

This is a game of luck for two people to play on a car journey. When you play, you will need to hold the book between you. You don't need counters for this game, just your fingers.

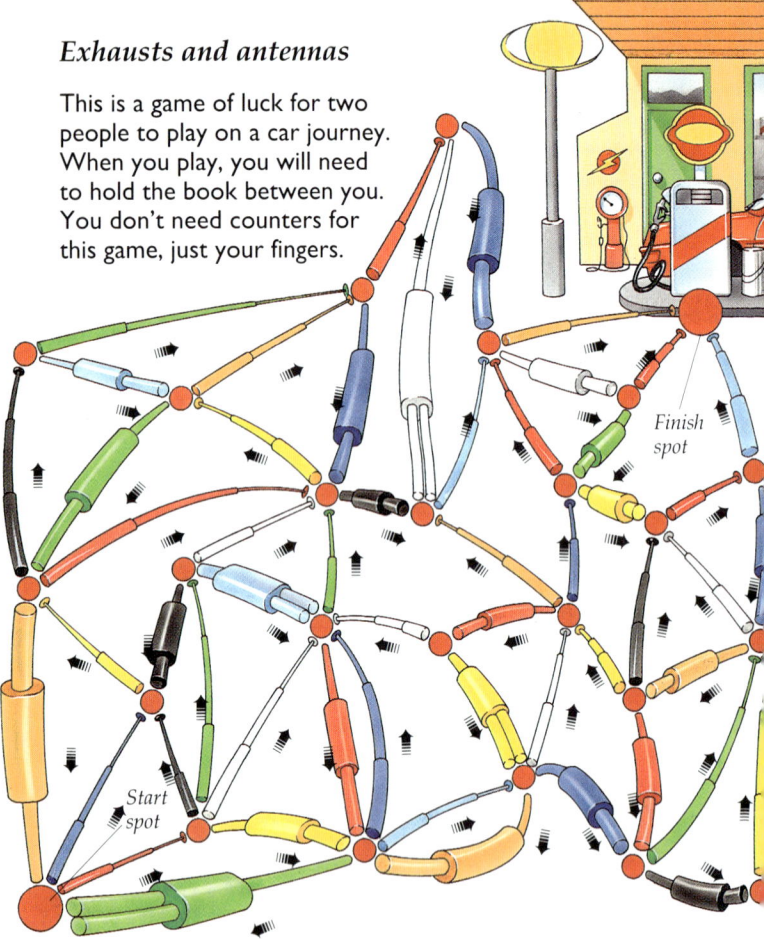

Finish spot

Start spot

How to play

1. Put your finger on the start spot nearest to you. As soon as you see a car with paint of a similar shade to a radio antenna leading from the start spot, move your finger up the antenna to the next spot.

2. Go up antennas or down exhausts, in the direction of the arrows, according to the paint on the cars you see. The first player to reach their finish spot at the fuel station is the winner. You could see who is the first to win three races.

Signpost game

On a road journey, have a competition to guess how long it will take to get from one signpost to the next. The person with the nearest guess is the winner.

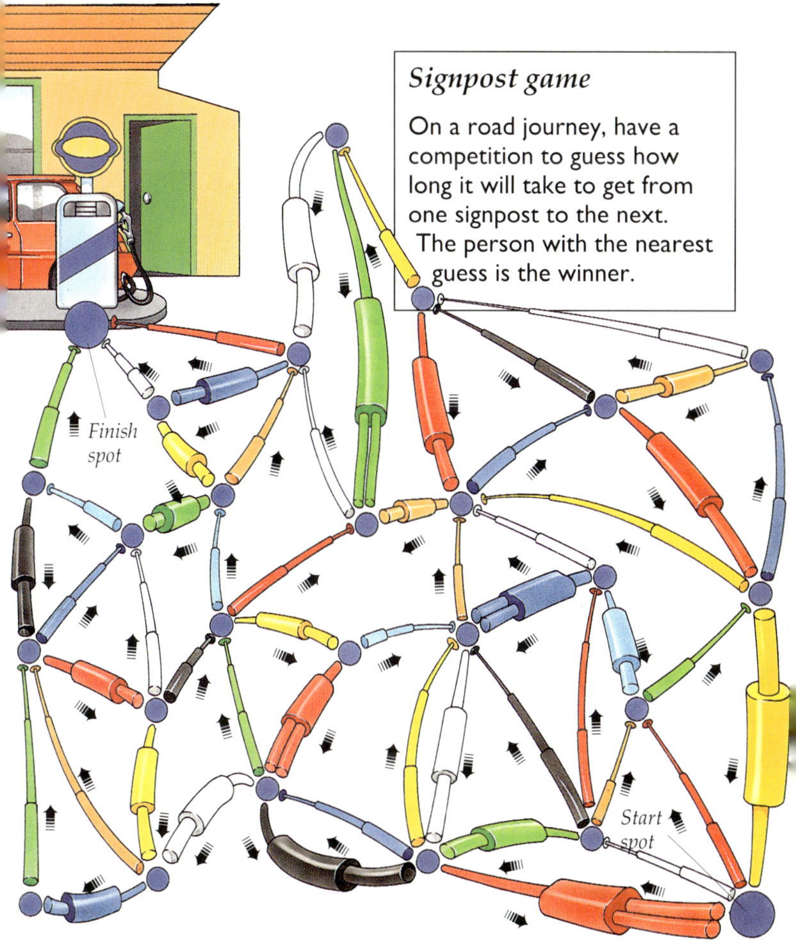

Finish spot

Start spot

Wheel puzzle

Six wheels are lined up as shown below. Can you re-arrange them to make the second pattern from the first, in just three moves?

In each move, move two wheels that are touching each other at the same time. Put them at either end of the row or in a gap.

Destination

This game is for two. Play it during a car journey, using counters*.

How to play

1. Stick your counter on one of the start squares. Then take turns spotting things from the score chart. Make up your own score chart if you like.

2. When you see an object that is on the score chart, move the number of squares indicated.

3. If you land on a white square, your next move must be in the direction shown by the arrow.

4. The bridges count as one square of the board.

5. The winner is the first to reach the other player's start square.

Making counters

To make counters for a game start by drawing small circles on stiff paper.

Carefully cut out the counters. Then draw on a design that suits the game.

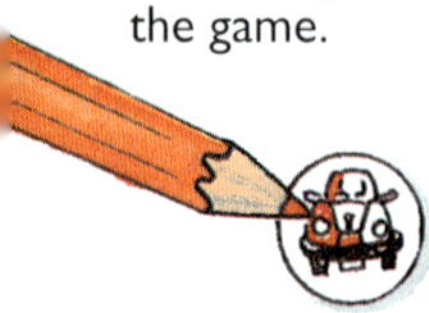

Decorate the counters differently so you can tell which counter belongs to which player.

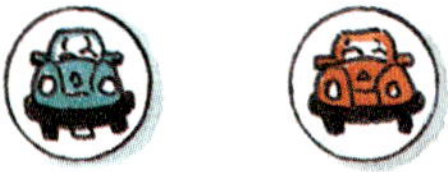

* *You'll need to stick your counters to the playing board with reusable adhesive, such as BLU-TACK™.*

Escape

Sam Snoop the spy is trying to escape from enemy agents. Unfortunately, they have set up road blocks everywhere. There is one route to safety across the border though. Which route should Sam take?

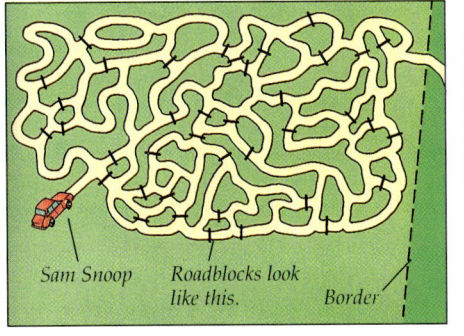

Sam Snoop
Roadblocks look like this.
Border

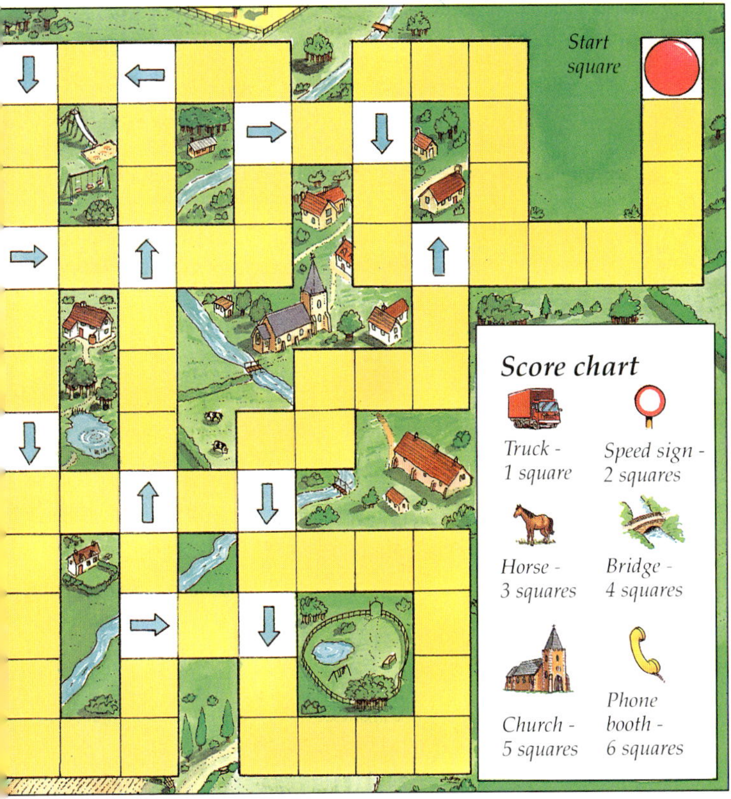

Start square
Score chart
Truck - 1 square
Speed sign - 2 squares
Horse - 3 squares
Bridge - 4 squares
Church - 5 squares
Phone booth - 6 squares

Car bingo

To play car bingo, make a card like the one below for each player, before the journey. The pictures on the cards show things to spot.

Each card should show the same things to spot, but in a different order. If you don't want to draw the pictures, simply write the names of the things in each square. The number of players is unlimited, but no two cards must be alike.

How to play

1. One person acts as the "caller", looking out of the car window to spot things from the card. As they call things out, the other players cross them off their cards.

2. The first person to get a horizontal or vertical line of crosses and shout out "Bingo!" is the winner. The card below shows both a vertical and horizontal line crossed off.

The big car quiz

1. Who made the first ever car?

   a. Karl Benz.
   b. Karl Cornerz.
   c. Henry Ford.

2. A race is held every year from Paris, France to which African town?

   a. Dundee, Scotland.
   b. Dhakar, Libya.
   c. Fez, Morocco.

3. What is an airbag?

   a. A chatty passenger.
   b. A safety device in a car.
   c. A special type of underwater car.

4. Which is the biggest selling car ever made?

   a. Volkswagen Beetle.
   b. Boeing 757.
   c. Fiat 500.

5. If you see a car with (BR) on its rear which country is it from?

   a. Great Britain.
   b. France.
   c. Brazil.

6. Which American car company made the Model T?

   a. Ford.
   b. Chrysler.
   c. Lincoln.

7. The first car radio in the world was installed in which Ford car?

   a. Model T.
   b. Mustang.
   c. Mustard.

8. In Brazil, some cars run on a fuel made from which of these?

   a. Vegetables.
   b. Soccer balls.
   c. Chocolate.

9. This was first heard in 1906. What is it?

   a. Electric car horn.
   b. Car radio.
   c. Noisy exhaust pipe.

10. In which state of the USA is the Indianapolis 500 race?

    a. Idaho.
    b. India.
    c. Indiana.

Puzzle answers

Treasure hunt (page 4-5)

The treasure is buried at Richman's Mansion.

If both cars travel at the same speed, the yellow car should get to the treasure first.

It is 300km (213 miles) from the yellow car's starting position to the treasure.

It is 320km (227 miles) from the red car's starting position to the treasure.

Buy a car for Sam Snoop (page 6)

Sam should buy Old Faithful. At top speed, it will get him to safety with 20 minutes to spare.

Decide the distance (page 6)

The blue car travels 4½km (3 miles) altogether.

Choose the route (page 7)

This is the route Parcel Pete should take to avoid going down any street more than once.

Fast Freddie's car (page 7)

Freddie spends 1,520 splots on spares for his car every 10,000km (6,000 miles).

Micky's rebuild (page 7)

The things that Micky left off his car when he rebuilt it are shown here.

Smuggler search (page 9)

Notorious Norbert is disguised as Shady Adey. His nose and mouth give away his identity.

Close up of Norbert. *Close up of Adey.*

Pyramid puzzler (page 11)

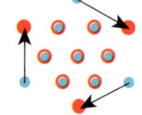

This is how the acrobats made the second pyramid (in red) from the first pyramid (in blue).

Sneaky spies (page 12-13)

This the route Sam Snoop should take.

Spot the spies (page 12)

There are eleven spies lurking at the airport.

Passport pieces (page 12)

Pieces A and D don't fit Madame LeRich's passport photograph.

The professor's prototypes (page 13)

Plane number 3 will have most trouble landing. It is the only plane without any wheels.

Plane maze (page 20)

The plane is directed to parking bay 3.

Parking problem (page 20)

Move the planes around in two steps, as shown here.

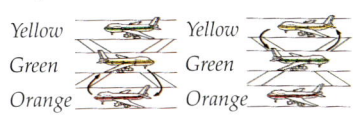

The great air quiz (page 21)

Answers:
1. b; 2. c; 3, a; 4. c; 5. c;
6. b; 7. c; 8. b; 9. a; 10. a.

Wheel puzzle (page 25)

Here is the sequence of moves to rearrange the wheels.

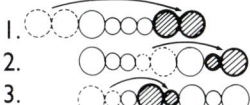

Escape (page 27)

This is the route Sam Snoop takes to get away from the enemy spies.

The big car quiz (page 29)

Answers:
1. a; 2. b; 3. b; 4. a; 5. c; 6. a;
7. a; 8. a; 9. a; 10. c.

How to make a scorer

If you don't have a dice you can make a scorer to use instead. To make one, you will need all of the things mentioned in the list on the right.

You will need:
Stiff plain paper; tracing paper; scissors; used match or something similar; pencil

1. Using the pencil, trace the shape and lines shown on the right onto tracing paper, as carefully as you can. Put the tracing face down on the stiff paper. Draw over the pencil marks with a pencil to transfer the tracing to the paper.

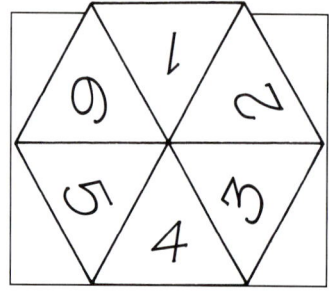

2. Carefully cut out the shape of the scorer from the stiff paper. Then mark one side with the numbers as shown in step 1.

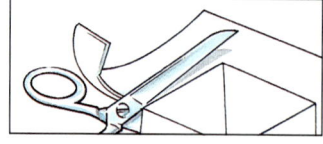

3. Make a small hole with a scissor point in the middle of the scorer. Then push the match through the scorer.

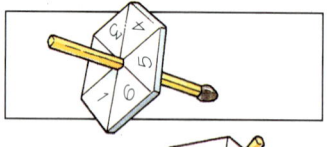

4. Spin the scorer around on a table, like a top. You score the number shown on the edge that comes to rest.

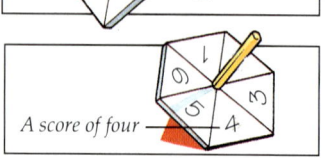

A score of four

This book is based on material previously published in *The Usborne Book of Air Travel Games* and *The Usborne Book of Car Travel Games*.
First published in 1996 by Usborne Publishing Ltd, Usborne House, 83-85 Saffron Hill, London EC1N 8RT, England.
Copyright © 1996, 1991, 1986, 1985 Usborne Publishing Ltd.
The name Usborne and the device 🎈 are Trade Marks of Usborne Publishing Ltd.
All rights reserved. No part of this publication may be reproduced, stored in a retrieval system or transmitted in any form or by any means, electronic, mechanical, photocopying, recording or otherwise, without the prior permission of the publisher.
First published in America August 1996 UE
Printed in Italy